MOTHER OF ANGELS

CONNOR WHITELEY

No part of this book may be reproduced in any form or by any electronic or mechanical means. Including information storage, and retrieval systems, without written permission from the author except for the use of brief quotations in a book review.

This book is NOT legal, professional, medical, financial or any type of official advice.

Any questions about the book, rights licensing, or to contact the author, please email connorwhiteley@connorwhiteley.net

Copyright © 2024 CONNOR WHITELEY

All rights reserved.

AUTHOR'S NOTE
Sections of this novella have previously appeared as Doctor Catherine Taylor short stories.

CHAPTER 1

The galaxy is a harsh, evil and deadly place for any species that dares to venture outside the natural orbit of its homeworld. Each year thousands of species in all the different galaxies in the universe venture out into the grand stars beyond, many die instantly because of how ill-prepared they are for the harshness of an uncaring galaxy. But every so often there is a species that makes it for a time at least.

Humanity was one of those them with a little help from the Emperor's superhuman warriors, the Angels of Death and Hope.

Doctor Catherine Taylor sat at her very posh slate-grey metal desk that hovered carefully in front of her as she switched off her holographic computer in her bright white office. She wasn't too fussed about the intense brightness of the almost glowing white walls, but it was her home for the time being.

She had to admit the little orbs of sheer light that hovered near the white ceiling was a great feature of the office, and it almost made her feel like she was back home on Earth with the Glorious Emperor, a definite god amongst men, but she had work to do here.

It had never ever mattered to Catherine how great the enviro-systems cleared, purified and scented the recycled air with hints of walnut and mint. Catherine was always going to know the smell of the real Emperor's palace that her own enviro-systems tried to manufacture. But the real smell was so intense that it actually left the taste of mint ice cream on her tongue.

This air did not.

Instead her mouth almost tasted dry with hints of oils, burnt ozone and iron forming on her tongue. It wasn't perfect, but she was just glad she was alive and safe and ready to work once more.

Catherine had always liked all the names she had been given by the different worlds and solar systems that belonged to the Great Human Empire. Some people called her Katie (but only her closest of friends which were very few in number). Others called her a crazy woman because of her determination to serve her Emperor that sometimes edged towards the illegal and others called her the Mother of Angels.

Catherine just smiled whenever she heard that name or reference aimed at her. Over 90,000 years ago, Catherine had helped the newly revealed Emperor of Humanity reunited Earth and then they set towards claiming the stars for humanity.

Even now Catherine didn't know why she exactly went along with the Emperor, but there was just something so charismatic, charming and god-like about him, that she just couldn't say no to him.

And after all, she was a Master of genetics, so she helped him to create the Angels of Death and Hope, and in a way she supposed she helped birth a new kind of human, one that could protect humanity in a very deadly galaxy.

Someone knocked on the metal door.

"Doctor Catherine," a man said.

Catherine rolled her eyes and with a flick of her wrist she commanded her office door to open. She already knew exactly who wanted to see her, it was the person in charge of this massive blade-like command cruiser.

Catherine had never been one for space travel too much because she was seeking an alien artifact in the system, and until she narrowed down what the artifact actually was, where it was located and how to get it. She was sadly stuck on the command ship until then, thankfully with her being so prized in the Empire, no one dared to disrupt her.

This man had balls.

"Doctor," the man said bowing his head.

Catherine nodded back to the man and really focused on him. He was wearing the black standard uniform of the very top commanders within a solar system's hierarchy, and like others she had seen before, his was covered with plenty of gold medals.

Including some medals showing he had fought side by side with her children, the Angels, and even fought against her traitorous children.

He was impressive to say the least, but none of it explained why he was here.

Catherine focused on his strong jawline, short brown hair and perfect posture. She couldn't help but wonder how his genes and what secrets they might help her with, she was even tempted to get a DNA sample, but that sort of illegal curiosity was why she had been sent away from Earth in the first place.

"I admit you are a lot more beautiful in the flesh than on my dataslate," the man said.

Catherine faked blushing, she had heard that all too much before. Men seemed to like her blond hair most of all and her model-like looks, that was one of the advantages of having the money and power she did, she could live for 90,000 years through medical treatments and rejuvenation treatments that she still managed to look great.

"Thank you commander…" Catherine said, gesturing him to reveal his name.

"I am Superior Commander Drax of the Samuel System named after the Supreme Rogue Trader himself that first discovered the system over 50,000 years ago," he said.

Catherine forced herself not to react, she had actually met the cock and he certainly didn't deserve a solar system named after him.

"You wish to speak with me about someone," Catherine said.

Drax nodded and leant closer to her. "You have experience with the Traitor Superhumans correct?"

Catherine gasped. She hadn't meant to but she hated all reminders that her glorious creations could be corrupted against the Emperor, herself and the Empire.

"I am," Catherine said. "Why?"

Drax frowned. "A very large fleet made of fifty traitor warships are coming into the system, and we have never dealt with a threat like this. We have requested aid but the nearest Angel detachment is six weeks away,"

Catherine smiled. She couldn't very well say the system was screwed but it basically was, yet that was why he had come to her. She had had battlefield experience, she had listened to the Emperor constantly about battle strategy and she had learnt tons over the past thousands of years.

If she couldn't help them then an entire solar system would die. Catherine wasn't having any of that.

CHAPTER 2

The last thing Catherine had been expecting was a massive oval chamber in the heart of the blade-like command ship with blinding bright walls, a large white oval table and little holograms of the planetary governors to round them, to serve as the meeting room.

Catherine had been expecting… well she was hardly sure but it hadn't been this. There were also tons of people that she certainly didn't like the look of.

She had met, kissed and killed a lot of military types over her lifetime, and the twenty different in-the-flesh people around the oval table just spelt trouble for her.

Catherine focused on a particular woman that summed up the military attitude towards the current crisis. She was a large muscular woman who was wearing a grey uniform, so she was probably from Navy Intelligence, basically a spy. Catherine was just amazed at how straight she sat, she looked like she was about to explode at any moment, but it wasn't with determination or anything.

Everyone at this table was so furious at the threat by the enemy that they actually looked reckless. And Catherine had had to deal with far too many reckless people in time, because reckless people were dangerous people.

And reckless people hardly listened to outsiders, especially one as rich as Catherine.

"My friends," Drax said as he sat down next to Catherine.

As Drax continued to introduce the threat, Catherine and the planetary governors and the members of the military command on the ship, Catherine just couldn't help but wonder why the traitors would attack this system.

It was no secret the Samuel system was a low priority system for the Empire. It was so far out in the galactic south that it was almost impossible to travel there quickly, even with the extreme speeds of modern technology, it had taken Catherine two years to travel here alone. She was impressed a tiny detachment (she had checked) of her children had been so close when the threat presented itself.

The snobbish reckless woman from Navy Intelligence stood up.

"I propose a full-conscription. We get every single man and woman on the planets regardless of age to be armed and enlisted," she said.

Catherine had talked with a few Navy officers in her time and that was strange for them. They were normally about countermeasures behind enemy lines, they weren't about open-conflict.

"No," Drax said. "We need people not in the army to fulfil the other industries and look after the children,"

The woman laughed. "What good is looking after the children if the traitors take the system?"

She did have a fair point but Catherine still wasn't sure. Forcing billions of people to take up arms was dangerous, especially as there were bound to be traitors infecting the population with hate, malice and corruption against the Emperor.

Arming them seemed futile, so Catherine told them.

"Doctor," one of the planetary governors said. "You are not a military specialist. You are not from here. You are not anything here,"

A good number of the other people at the table nodded.

Catherine just smiled. She had had to deal with these idiots a lot and they were always as stupid as each other. Humans were almost as stupid 90,000 years ago as they were today.

The oval table hummed a little as a massive hologram of the Samuel system revealed itself showing the first of the traitor warships entering the system.

The warships would reach the first planet within hours and the four billion people on that planet would die.

Catherine watched the other military commanders pretend to study the details but they had no clue what they were facing.

"We must evacuate the planet," someone said.

"There is no time!" a woman shouted, presumably the planetary governor of the world.

The military commanders in the room simply shrugged. They didn't care and those soldiers on the planet probably didn't even know how to fire a gun let alone kill a superhuman.

Four billion people were going to die unless Catherine did something.

Catherine stood up. "I have listened to the Emperor himself talk and if you don't do as exactly as I say, your system will burn. Every single person in this solar system will be ash if you don't listen to me,"

Catherine wasn't exactly sure what her grand plan would be but she was just hoping to buy herself some time and hopefully her threats or reminders of the danger would trigger some sort of response.

"We need to run," an elderly military commander said.

Catherine had hoped he was joking first of all but the other military commanders and planetary governors were nodding in total agreement.

"And where will we go?" Drax asked.

"I suggest we vote on the matter now," the Navy Intelligence woman said.

Everyone else but Drax nodded.

Catherine just looked at Drax for a moment and realised that he might be the person officially in charge here, he probably had more real military experience than the rest of the people in the meeting combined.

But he had no real power.

The hologram of the system flashed red as more and more fleets of the traitors turned up and zoomed towards the first planet.

Catherine was never going to tell the military commanders in the room that each fleet would be made up of five ships carrying five thousands soldiers each. That was twenty-five thousand superhumans in a fleet and there was a lot more than one coming towards them.

It still made no sense why so many were coming to this system of all things.

Catherine just knew as she saw the anger behind Drax's eyes that he was an outsider. He wasn't born in the system and this solar system had never seen any real conflict, so what do people do when they've faced a life of easy-living and no hardship?

They simply run away when hardship comes.

Catherine laughed aloud, not because she, completely, despised the military of this solar system for its cowardice and willingness to give up the Emperor's land to foul traitors. But because she actually wanted to save them.

"Stop," Catherine said, standing up. "Have you ever faced the enemy in battle?"

Everyone but Drax put at their hands in their laps.

"Have you ever faced the traitor, the alien or the mutant?" Catherine asked.

No answer.

If Catherine was on any other world she might have cursed, damned or just ordered these people to be stripped of their rank. A thankful thing she had the power to do thanks to the divine Emperor's trust in her.

But she wouldn't.

"If you all agree to fight then I will make you something I haven't worked on for 80,000 years," Catherine said.

Everyone gasped.

Catherine had worked on the superhuman Angels of Death and Hope for thousands of years as she had perfected the process and now other minds worked on it, and Catherine researched other matters to help humanity.

But if it meant saving billions of lives then Catherine was willing to make some superhumans once more. She always carried the equipment with her just in case but it was still a massive risk.

Not just legally but ethically too.

Everyone looked at her strangely even Drax.

"What's your price?" Drax asked.

Catherine gave him an evil grin because he clearly knew her reputation beyond the official records and her illegal curiosity. She would have asked this later on from Drax after the battle was won but she might as well collect it now.

"I need you to tell me what the traitors are after. They did not come here for the fun of it. I too seek an artifact but I don't know what it looks like, what it does or anything. I just know I have to find something," Catherine said.

The commanders' eyes flickered at each other as if they wanted someone to tell Catherine she was wrong or to get the hell out of their system.

But they were desperate and reckless. Something that was critical in these moments.

Drax slowly nodded. "The system is home to an artifact known as the Keystone. It is a small diamond-like object made from metal, we don't know what it does but we keep on the capital world,"

Catherine nodded her thanks to Drax for telling her. If she wasn't such a good person that was so obsessed with the Empire and the Emperor, then she couldn't lie that she was tempted to just leave them, go to the capital world and get this *Keystone* before the system was a hulk of wasteland.

But she loved protecting innocent people too much.

"I need as many people under 50 Earth-standard-years as you can get me. They must be willing and evacuation orders must be sent to the first two planets the traitors will hit," Catherine said.

Deadly silence descended across the meeting room but Drax was already sending the orders to the crew and the first two planets.

Catherine had no idea if she could create Angels so quickly after so many decades but she had to try.

She had to try to save as many lives as she could.

CHAPTER 3

About two days later she sat back in her very spacious bright white office watching the little orbs of light hover near the ceiling as she rested her hands on her hovering desk. She had worked flat out over the past 48 hours to convert the crew people she had been sent into Angels.

Catherine had actually forgotten how amazing it felt to rip a large chunk of a person's DNA out, twist it and mix it with other genes from different sources to create a concoction that would start the process.

As much as Catherine hated it that she didn't have the organs, specialised equipment and a full Genetics Team next to her. She had still done a lot better than she had ever imagined.

Catherine switched on her holographic computer to watch her new creations board the warships that would carry them into battle.

Unlike normal Angels that were over 9 feet tall, faster and stronger than the typical human along with carrying thick armour and an immense gun that could bring an entire building crashing down with a single shot. These Angels were more humble and mortal than her blessed creations from all those thousands of years ago.

But these Angels might not have been as strong, immortal and lacking all the organs that gave the normal Angels special abilities that baseline-humans could only dream of.

They were still stronger, tougher and deadlier than the normal human soldiers that would be shattered by the traitors, so there was a hope.

A hope that billions of lives could be saved because of Catherine's intervention.

Catherine really wished she could race back to Earth right now and continue with her genetic work, getting back to what she truly loved, but she wasn't done in the Samuel system yet.

If the traitors were after this *Keystone* then Catherine was more than willing to hunt it down too. She had to find it for the divine Emperor and she had to have it for her research.

No matter her findings, no matter how many laws she broke in the quest for knowledge, Catherine would do it.

Not because she hated the Empire and wanted to punish it by breaking law after law but because she loved it too much.

Catherine loved it so much that she would do whatever it took to save it from the traitors and aliens and mutants, no matter who got caught in the fire of her determination.

CHAPTER 4

During all 90,000 years of her long life, Catherine absolutely had to admit she had never been in such an interestingly awful place in her entire life.

Catherine stood in the dead-centre of a very long rectangular room with the ugliest brown wooden flooring with little flecks of something that she really didn't want to know too much about. It was probably some kind of mould, but that was the last thing she wanted to consider.

The ugly flooring was such a strange contrast to the absolutely delightfully bright white ceiling with little shards of technology humming quietly as they strained themselves to create the almost blinding effect.

Even the gentle smells of lemon, thyme and ginger was a signal that the enviro-systems were malfunctioning and not recycling the air correctly. In fact Catherine was fairly sure she was the first person to visit the Samuel System's national museum for quite some time, judging by the thick layer of dust that covered the U-shaped glass cabinets.

Catherine had had a quick look at the other

cabinets when she first got here but they were ugly, and at least from her viewpoint, as the geneticist and so-called Mother of the Emperor's superhuman Angels of Death and Hope, were pretty pointless.

All Catherine had seen were some shards of pottery, a very lame engine of the first shuttle to land on a planet in the Samuel System and there was even a perfectly preserved finger belonging to the cock of the Rogue Trader that first discovered the system fifty thousand years ago.

Catherine was hardly impressed but then in a way she had never been interested in those other artifacts, because right in front of her in the very centre of the room she was in, was Catherine's true prize.

Catherine just stared at the stunning triangular metal device that was perfectly tall at 20cm as it was wide, and it was no deeper than Catherine's hand. It was a rather small triangular device made completely from a strange(ish) type of silver metal that pulsed with blue energy every minute or so.

Of all the things she had been felt the need to search for in her long life, she hadn't been expecting this, because for the first time in her existence she had no idea what this actually was.

All she knew was that she had had a strong urge to travel to the Samuel System and find an artifact. This was the artifact she had been wanting to seek, now she only needed to know what it did.

"Is this what you seeked?" a man asked as his heavy footsteps pounded across the ugly floor towards her.

Catherine nodded and instantly knew that it was the person in charge of the entire military inside the Samuel System, Commander Drax.

Catherine had to admit he was a good man, and a very clever man too. He had known to seek her out when his system had been under-attack by superhuman traitors (or her traitorous children as she called them behind closed doors), and she had helped him.

In return he helped her by telling Catherine where the artifact was.

"I'm glad, and please take the Keystone. No one visits here anyway," Drax said.

Catherine smiled at him, and tried to forget about his eyes that were so focused on her breasts and her short blond hair. But she couldn't understand why he kept calling it a Keystone, ever since she had told him about the relic he had referred to it as a Keystone.

Yet one thing was sadly clear, Catherine's traitorous children were attacking the system so they could get it. So Catherine had to find out what the hell was going on with it no matter what happened.

She didn't feel like she had another option and that both excited and terrified her.

ANGELS OF MOTHER

CHAPTER 5

Catherine was more than relieved it didn't take the stuck-up museum owner long to just give her the Keystone. She hated how the museum man doubted her abilities to solve such a complex mystery considering even *he* of all people couldn't solve it.

Catherine had borrowed one of the only universities in Samuel system's science labs. Even that was a harsh term to describe nothing more than a long bright grey room with a few pieces of machinery to run tests and a long sterile white metal table for examinations.

It wasn't exactly the best equipment or lab she had ever been in, but Catherine was far too concerned at the moment to risk taking the Keystone out of the system. The Samuel System might have been under attack from her children but at least she was somewhat protected.

And even if her children did manage to make it to the capital world of the system, she would still have enough time to escape. Catherine's only fear of escaping with the Keystone was that she doubted she would have the military backup in case she was followed and hunted down.

That definitely wasn't a good idea.

Catherine forced herself to focus on the wonderfully cold triangular Keystone under her white gloved hands. Catherine didn't know where to begin so she went back to basics.

The small pentagonal door behind her opened, Catherine just rolled her eyes as Commander Drax walked in.

"I am capable of investigating this myself Commander," Catherine said.

"I do not doubt that but I am Commander of this system and I would like to know if this is an advantage over the enemy," Drax said.

Catherine wanted to argue but she simply went over to the range of machinery and managed to find a little scanning device that was no bigger than her palm.

She went back over to it and just hoped beyond hope it would reveal something as she started scanning it.

But as the little scanner studied the Keystone, it came up completely empty almost like there wasn't even an object in front of her.

That was beyond weird and Catherine had only encountered objects like this a few times. And none of them had been easy to study, Catherine loved a challenge.

Catherine went back over to the range of machinery and really smiled when she found the lab had what looked like the very first model of a Molecular Studier. Which Catherine always described to undergraduates (because the truth was so complex) as a little screwdriver device that touches an object and gives you a very advance breakdown of what it's made from.

Catherine went back over to the Keystone, touched it with the screwdriver device and the device went through the Keystone.

"Interesting," Catherine said to herself.

The smell of vanilla ice cream filled the air and formed on Catherine's tongue, and it was starting to become crystal clear that something flat out weird was going on.

It was clear as day that technology didn't work on the Keystone, but then Catherine couldn't have imagined the stuck-up museum man being as arrogant as he was unless he had had at least some luck studying the object.

Unless of course he was just too prideful to imagine a mere outsider could do better than him. The sad truth was that he might actually be right.

"Damn it," Drax said.

Catherine looked at him briefly and gestured him to explain what he meant.

"It's the traitors. They just destroyed an entire fleet of my forces," Drax said.

Catherine bit her lip. She had monitored the traitor attack closely and out of the twelve planets in the Samuel System, two had had to be evacuated whilst Catherine used her genetic knowledge to create some crude Superhumans to help Drax defend his system, and another one had been lost to the traitors.

Catherine couldn't allow yet another planet to fall.

It quickly dawned on Catherine that she was actually going about this investigation all wrong, she had been too focused on technology instead of what she used to do before she met the Emperor all those tens of thousands of years ago and used her genetic knowledge to help him. She used to study the remains of human cultures even during the time when the Tech-barbarians enslaved humanity (she was one of the handful of people who had managed to remain free throughout) and before the Emperor freed them all.

Each time she came across a human remain, she didn't use technology, she used her hands and actually focused on what *she* could see, touch and learn.

Catherine carefully took off her gloves, hating every second of it as it went against every single rule and fibre of her scientific being, and she slowly touched the Keystone.

Her hands went icy cold, the Keystone lit up bright fiery red and Catherine felt something build within it.

Red energy shot out.

Throwing Catherine against the wall.

Drax slammed next to her.

The lights went off and emergency red lights activated. Catherine had no idea what just happened and Drax kept swearing under his breath.

"The entire planet has lost power. The ships and defenders in the void and on other planets cannot relay with us. They're on their own. The traitors could kill them all and we would have no idea," Drax said.

Catherine gasped. She hadn't meant for that to happen. She hadn't meant for any of this but she had done something extremely dangerous and deadly.

Something she had to fix. She just had absolutely no idea how to solve it.

CHAPTER 6

Normal people might have panicked, screamed or been frozen by fear as the emergency red lightning inside the little "lab" beamed down on them, but Catherine wasn't just a human, she was apparently one of the brightest minds in the entire history of humanity, save maybe the Emperor himself.

But as she stood over the triangular Keystone, she really didn't feel like it.

"Does anything work on the planet?" Catherine asked.

Drax's frown worsened and Catherine just wanted to smile at him. It was just so typical of humans to get so emotional and angry in times like this instead of acting rationally and working towards getting the real job done.

"Negative. All generators are offline. All defences are offline and estimates are the engineers cannot get the generators working for another week. We can only slightly communicate because the emergency power,"

Catherine had to admit it was damn well impressive that a system as unloved and forgettable as the Samuel System still had access to backup power. Some of the really unremarkable systems she had travelled to barely had that, or didn't at all.

Catherine stared at the relic once more and carefully traced her fingers over its icy cold metal surface. This was the strangest object she had ever seen.

The Keystone sparkled with electrical sparks popping off it before getting reabsorbed into the strange metal.

Catherine looked at Drax. "It seems the Keystone has stolen all the power on the planet,"

Drax huffed. "Each second power is out is another second our troops don't have orders and we cannot react to the enemy's movements,"

Catherine just shook her head. This was exactly one of the reasons why she created the Angels of Death and Hope in the first place, her superhumans were so powerful, capable and deadly that they didn't need orders from another planet to know what to do. Their training taught them exactly how to react in this situation and win.

Catherine just smiled as she quickly realised that those crude Angels she had made for the systems were hardly true Angels. Normal superhumans had hundreds of hours of training before they were released onto the battlefield. These Angels had none of it.

"Surely if the Keystone took the power," Catherine said. "It should be able to release it and return it to your planet,"

Drax came over to her. Catherine wasn't a fan of how close he was with his heavy breathing on her neck but given how dire the situation was, this wasn't the time for personal space concerns.

Catherine grabbed the Keystone.

Nothing happened. Catherine couldn't understand why the artifact wasn't working this time before whenever she touched it, it would-

Black energy shot up. An immense shockwave was unleashed.

Throwing Catherine against the wall.

Drax just stood there.

Catherine stood up but she was surprised she didn't feel any pain whatsoever, and now she was actually thinking about it she couldn't remember hitting the wall either. It was like the Keystone had wanted to throw her against the wall but not to hurt her.

That was another strange thing.

The emergency power went out.

Catherine heard the door lock itself and Drax huffed as presumably his communicator was deactivated.

Now the entire capital world of the Samuel System was alone, isolated and dead in the water.

The traitors could appear in high orbit and no one would know they needed to mount a defence. By the time Catherine and Drax left the lab the entire world could be ash.

Catherine folded her arms in the pitch darkness. "Clearly the Keystone wants energy but why?"

Drax sounded like he was throwing his arms up in the air. "Like I know. Doctor I have given you everything and all you seem to be doing is destroying my planet,"

Catherine couldn't exactly argue with him there.

"My planet, my system, my people could be dead

because of you," Drax said.

"Be quiet," Catherine said.

The strangest thing of this entire experience was that Catherine just knew the entire lab was pitch black but to her at least the Keystone was glowing a very faint blue.

"Do you see the Keystone glowing?" Catherine asked.

"No," Drax said.

Catherine went to touch it but everything single time she had done that something awful had happened. And as much as she didn't want to imagine it the only source of energy left on the planet was the life force inside the billions of people on the world.

She couldn't kill them.

That almost made her laugh. She had basically created superhuman killing machines that continued to kill the enemies of her divine Emperor and burn entire solar systems but she was hesitant to kill an entire world.

That almost made no sense to the scientist in her.

"Drax," Catherine said, hating herself for how vulnerable her voice sounded. "I want to touch the Keystone again but I don't know what will happen,"

"Command it," Drax said.

Even though Catherine realised that Drax's voice wasn't his own. It was a strange form of his voice but it was too high and too deep at the same time. It was like something had replaced Drax or at least entered his body.

"Who is this?" Catherine asked.

CHAPTER 7

"The Keystone or the Intelligence that powers it," the thing inside Drax said.

Catherine wanted to ask so many questions, she had so many possibilities and experiments she wanted to run but she had to focus on the mission. Something that was hardly easy with the damn red emergency lighting covering the white lab in a horrible red glow.

Catherine just had to restore the power to the planet and save lives.

"How do I release the power?" Catherine asked.

"Doctor Catherine Taylor," the Intelligence said, "one of the best minds in the Empire doesn't know what I am, who I am or what I can do,"

Then Catherine realised that the Intelligence was right she was one of the best minds in the Empire and she needed to channel her past experience.

About 60,000 years ago she had been on a moon of a massive gas giant and she had encountered an artifact with a similar power. Except this one managed to knock out the communication systems only in the entire system, and it wasn't during a conflict, she had managed to reverse it.

Catherine just looked at where the Intelligence was standing and picked up the small screwdriver device that she had placed next to the Keystone.

She raised it up like she was going to strike it.

That's how she had managed to reverse the effects of the artifact on that moon, she had threatened it. Clearly whatever had knocked out the communications systems had a pretty strong sense of survival.

The Intelligence laughed.

"I learnt from your last attempt. Technology cannot hurt me and I will destroy your power," the Intelligence said.

Catherine couldn't believe that she was facing the same enemy as before but maybe that was the key.

Catherine just focused on the Keystone and truly focused on herself as a cold rational scientist.

This was an object made from an alien metal that seemed to suck out the power of a planet and store it for an unknown purpose. The sucking ability seemed to be activated by touch and it-

That was it. Catherine knew all she had to do was made sure that someone else touched it because everything seemed to be focused on her touch. It was her touch that powered it.

She had to get Drax or the Intelligence to touch it. She didn't know why she felt like that but she just knew deep inside her that that was the key to everything.

Catherine put on her white gloves again and felt out to see where Drax's body was standing.

"What are you doing?" the Intelligence asked.

Catherine kept feeling until she reached his hand

and she grabbed his wrist.

"Let me go," the Intelligence said.

Catherine loved the hint of fear in its voice.

Catherine pulled his arm hard. Forcing his hand to touch the Keystone.

The Intelligence resisted. It was strong. Catherine kept pulling.

"Harder!" Drax himself shouted.

Drax's body surged forward. His hand touching the Keystone.

The Intelligence screamed in agony and popped and banged.

The Keystone glowed bright white.

Blinding white energy shot out. Pulling Catherine closer.

Then the lights turned back on and Catherine just hoped that power to the entire planet was restored, and as she closed down at the smoking remains of Drax's arm she feared the worse.

Then Drax moved his head, his eyes blinked and he just focused on the smouldering remains of his arm.

Catherine wasn't sure what had just happened but she was determined to find out.

CHAPTER 8

As much as Catherine hated the arrogant idiot of the museum man he sadly had friends in the highest offices of the System's government, friends so powerful that even Drax, with his new cybernetic arm, couldn't overrule them.

Catherine stood back in the museum room where this latest nightmare had started with its ugly brown wooden floors, rather wonderful bright white ceiling and U-shape ring of glass cabinets filled with useless pieces of the system's past.

Catherine just stared at the humming, buzzing and crackling Keystone that was inside a glass cabinet in front of her.

Thankfully Catherine had managed to find out exactly what had caused the problems, it seemed that the Keystone was most definitely alien in nature and contained some sort of Artificial Intelligence that seemed to be able to spread from one Keystone to another.

Catherine had no idea that she had found a Keystone-like object 60,000 years ago, and even now she still wasn't sure what had happened to it. But at least there was only one Artificial Intelligence in the entire network of Keystone, otherwise surely she would have seen more than one Intelligence.

That was a logical and rational assumption to her at least.

Catherine had even worked out a possible scenario to why Drax had been corrupted or "possessed" (as the laypeople would put it), Drax was the only person in the room that was weak enough for the Intelligence to get ahold of. Clearly something made it impossible for the Intelligence to capture herself so Catherine supposed that Drax was the next best thing.

But why did it respond to her touch? What was its purpose and why did she feel like there was more in the Samuel System that she just had to find out about?

"Doctor," Drax said as he walked in behind her.

Catherine turned around and smiled at the Commander. She would never show it but she was glad that he was okay and getting on with his cybernetic arm okay, some people seriously struggled.

"I wanted to let you know," Drax said, "that your stunt didn't cost lives. Your Angels were very clever and took immediate control of the situation and we are currently pushing the Traitor forces back,"

Catherine smiled that was good news, but she didn't have the heart to tell him she hadn't really cared overly about if her "stunt" had costed lives.

She had learnt so much and now she had a firmer understanding of the Keystone that any cost was worth it in her quest for knowledge.

"And in the interest of being fair to you," Drax said. "When this planet blacked out, there was another planet that did the same for no reason that our people can understand,"

Catherine took a few steps closer. "Really?"

Drax nodded. "It seems even now there is an energy signal pulsing in space with the same energy signature as the Keystone behind you when we first discovered it,"

Catherine smiled. That was excellent news and that was where she had to go next but she already guessed by the concerned look on Drax's face that it was on a planet that was right in the Traitor's warpath.

"I know you will go and I will go with you personally," Drax said. "The traitors seem to be sending an entire fleet, so 25,000 troops in total to the planet. Still want to go?"

Catherine just smiled. Drax might have been an amazing commander, clever and a damn good man, but his mind was so small compared to Catherine's and the Emperor's.

She knew that some people would see her as cold, distant and calculating but she had been fighting the war to make sure humanity survived for tens of thousands of years. She had learnt to forget about the *one-lives* long ago, if a few little mortals died in her quest for knowledge and to save humanity, then so be it.

CHAPTER 9

Bright crystal shards showered down upon the crisp hard desert ground with bright impressive streaks of yellow, pink and purple in the sand that made the world appear as alien as anything Doctor Catherine Taylor had ever seen. She might have been around for over 90,000 years because of her artificial genetics, medical advancements and rejuvenation treatments, but even this planet was a wonder to her.

Catherine stood perfectly still on a massive, almost endless, desert in the middle of nowhere as the little crystal shards showered down on her long blue trench coat and bounced off her velvety blond hair, when she had wanted to come to this planet to search for an artifact that had been releasing an energy signal, almost calling out to her, she hadn't expected the world to look like this.

The field was completely flat with only the yellow, pink and purple grains of sand adding any texture, colour or something to see to the ground. There was no wind but somehow the grains of sand swirled, twirled and moved along the ground like there was a current that Catherine couldn't feel.

Catherine was even more interested in why there was such a strong scent of dried apricots that seemed so out of place considering the nearest trees were over a hundred kilometres away in the world's capital city. That was desperately preparing itself for an incoming invasion.

As much as Catherine wanted, needed to stay on the world in the backwater and unloved and forgettable Samuel System, she just knew that she couldn't stay here any longer than necessary.

The distant roar of cannon firing made Catherine just frown as she realised that the superhumans she had forged, created and basically became a mother to where here. If these were the loyal superhuman Angels of Death and Hope then maybe she would have smiled. But it was her traitorous children that were the attackers today, so if she didn't hurry up and find the artifact she seek then she would have to face her children.

And she didn't like her odds. She was a baseline human, her children were stronger, tougher and deadlier than anything she could have ever imagined when she first started the project with the Glorious Emperor all those tens of thousands of years ago.

"Doctor," Commander Drax said behind her.

Catherine rolled her eyes. The last thing she had ever needed was a babysitter but considering he was in charge of the system's military, he was a good and powerful ally to have.

Catherine looked at him and smiled at his strong jawline, solid muscular body and rather beautiful eyes. Drax just stared at her, and Catherine was starting to wonder how badly did he want to run his dirty fingers through her silky blond hair.

Catherine definitely wasn't going to allow that to ever happen.

The loud rumble overhead made Catherine look up and she slowly nodded as she saw a two-kilometre-long blue blade-like battle cruiser descend towards them.

"This is the only ship I can spare your little adventure," Drax said. "I will remain here until you and the Artifact are safely secured,"

Catherine didn't know how to take that, she wasn't some mere object to be secured and transported, she was a human. But she smiled anyway.

Slowly Catherine took out a small metal fork-like object that was constantly scanning the strange rainbow-coloured ground in search of the energy signals that she was looking for.

This entire hunt had started so long ago when she had first felt the urge to travel to the silly Samuel system, it had taken her two years to get there but at least she had found the first artifact, a Keystone as Drax and the natives called it.

That Keystone had only left more questions than answers and something when she had activated the Keystone only yesterday, it had activated something on this planet that was pulsing intense energy into the cold deadly void of space.

That was exactly what Catherine wanted to find out.

The little scanner in her hand vibrated slightly as she slowly walked around the area.

It vibrated more and more before the scanner popped and smoke poured out. Crystal shards slowly showered the wreckage of the scanner before it simply sunk into the strange grains of the sand.

Catherine pointed over to Drax and he radioed the cruiser overhead to send down a military detachment to start the excavation.

As Catherine just stared down on the spot of ground at her feet she felt butterflies fill her stomach. She always felt like this whenever she was about to make a discovery.

She had no idea what was below the surface but she couldn't wait to find out.

Catherine just had a feeling it was going to change the course of the war and the fate of the Samuel system.

CHAPTER 10

A few hours later Catherine stood at the very edge of a massive hole and stared down tens of metres towards the bottom where marines were powering cranes and other technology in an effort to find the treasure that she sought.

Catherine had conducted a few tests on the strange yellow, pink and purple sand that seemed to be moving faster around the hole they were digging but the sand did not fall into the hole, killing the men and women inside.

Catherine had wondered if the sand would do that at some point but from the tests that she had run, the sand seemed to repel any touch with organic matter. Granted that didn't explain in the slightest how she and Drax were standing right next to each other without the sand parting.

But that could simply be because her and Drax were wearing combat boots, and because of the rather extreme heat inside the hole the marines were occasionally digging with their bare hands, and walking round in bare feet.

It was a theory and whilst the marines dug, it

wasn't like Catherine had anything else to do.

Distant roars, booms and explosions ripped across the wide endless field or space (Catherine wasn't really sure what to call it) and she just knew that time was running out. Sooner or later her traitorous children would be here, and would try to take the artifact from her.

"What do you think it is?" Drax asked.

Catherine shrugged. In the past few hours she had actually learnt to respect Drax's mind a little, it was clever, curious and maybe in another life he could have been a great scientist instead of a military commander. But that ship had sailed about a hundred years ago.

"Another Keystone perhaps," Catherine said.

It was the most logical answer, but Catherine nervously moved her hands together as she still knew the icy coldness of the metal triangular Keystone she had studied on the Samuel System's Capital World unleashed all that destruction.

She just hoped this artifact wouldn't do the same.

"Doctor!" someone shouted.

Catherine looked down the hole again and saw something rising up.

The hole collapsed.

Drax threw Catherine to one side.

Catherine fell back.

The sand shifted. Sealing the hole up.

Catherine jumped up. Drax was gone. All those marines were trapped in the sand. What had Catherine done?

The sand where the hole had been moved and shifted and Catherine rushed over. Digging with her hands as much as the sand as she could.

"Drax!" she shouted.

Catherine kept digging. She felt a hand. She pulled it up. She sunk ankle-deep into the sand.

She didn't care.

Catherine kept pulling.

She pulled up a female marine who helped her to dig more and more.

Catherine grabbed another hand. She pulled them up. The female marine pulled up someone too.

There was still no sign of Drax.

The entire ground shook slightly and the sand moved dramatically.

Catherine fell to the ground, caught up in the constant current of the moving yellow, purple and pink sand.

The landscape changed as Catherine was pulled by an invisible current. The field was no longer flat or endless.

When the sand stopped moving twenty corpses of suffocated marines surrounded Catherine as she realised she was inside a bright yellow, purple and pink crater.

"Help," Drax said.

Catherine looked around and saw that Drax's head was poking out of the ground and she quickly pulled him up.

Thankfully another ten marines had managed to pull themselves out of the sandy ground, but Catherine just wanted to focus for a moment on all the dead round her.

She was a geneticist by training and she couldn't help but wonder how the genes of the silly dead marines had helped in their damnation and death. Of course the main cause of their deaths was the artifact and sand (environmental factors) but they had to have interacted with the genetics somehow to-

"Doctor," Drax said, as he turned his communicator to loudspeaker.

"Is everything okay Commander?" the woman Captain of the cruiser asked.

"Affirmative Captain Ella," Drax said. "What happened from your perspective?"

"Enemy forces are gaining ground. Two capital class destroyers are annihilated and two strike forces of enemy superhumans have made planetfall, and the energy signals from the artifact have deactivated,"

Catherine hadn't ever wanted to consider the way the battle was going, that was foul enough, but the artifact had deactivated itself. Why?

From what she had discovered from the Keystone on the capital world, it was clear that they wanted power, regardless of its source. But unlike the capital world the artifact hadn't knocked out the planet's power or communication systems.

Why not?

"Captain," Catherine said, "Were your marines wearing body cameras when they died?"

Catherine almost smiled at the sound of the Captain moving uncomfortably at the reminder of the deaths.

"Confirmed Doctor Playing footage now," Captain Ella said.

"Thank you," Catherine said.

Drax's communicator hummed for a moment before holographic images of the artifact appeared.

"Pause," Catherine said.

The hologram image paused and Catherine just saw a massive triangular object with sizes all the same

length, probably four metres tall, made from a strange glowing black metal that Catherine had seen a few times before but never this far in the galactic south and there was a crystal inside.

From the image it looked like a massive diamond but Catherine couldn't be sure unless she examined it more closely.

Then Catherine realised that the Keystone on the capital world seemed to connect to her somehow, and it only worked when she touched it.

Catherine knelt down on the ground and placed her palm on the surprisingly cold sand and it all stopped moving around them.

"Come to me," Catherine said.

The entire ground shook. The sand crater collapsed around them.

Sand collapsed round Catherine's head. She didn't dare breathe. The sand tried to invade her ears, nose and her mouth.

Catherine didn't let it.

The sand almost roared in her ears. Catherine needed air. She was struggling to breathe.

The sand dragged her further down.

Catherine felt herself stop. Then the sand threw her upwards.

She didn't dare scream.

Catherine was thrown into the air leaving the sandy grave behind her.

When Catherine landed on the cold sand on her backside, she quickly stood up and her mouth dropped as the massive three-metre-tall triangular keystone was right in front of her.

"Doctor," Drax said, fear edged his voice.

Catherine looked at him briefly and noted how

few marines were left around them.

"Call in more forces from the cruiser. We need to get the artifact out of here before the enemy comes," Catherine said coldly.

Drax hesitated for a moment almost like he didn't really want the Large Keystone on his ship. Thankfully Catherine couldn't have cared less about what he wanted, she was on a quest for her glorious Emperor and to save humanity.

There was nothing more important than that goal.

"Of course," Drax said as he radioed it in.

Catherine went over to the Artifact and it seemed to pulse softly at her like she was a friend that it was happy to see once again.

"Please don't do anything dangerous," Catherine said quietly to the Artifact.

Little did she realise just how bad things were about to get.

CHAPTER 11

The pulsing slowly and became even friendlier so Catherine supposed that the Artifact was agreeing with her, and hopefully making a promise.

A loud bang and humming overhead made Catherine smile as massive bird-like shuttles descended towards them. Catherine backed away from the shuttle as smaller grey blade-like shuttles descended too.

The bird-like shuttles were definitely for the transportation of the Artifact, because the cruiser was far too big to land and quickly escape with the Artifact, the blade-like shuttles were filled with military support.

The largest of the bird-like shuttles was just beautiful and Catherine was more than looking forward to riding in it with the Artifact.

It exploded.

Flaming chunks of wreckage smashed into the sand.

The Artifact glowed bright red.

Catherine looked at the sky. Tens of massive black blade-like shuttles were zooming towards them.

The enemy had come.

The enemy opened fired.

Drax tackled Catherine to the ground.

The bird-like shuttles were annihilated. Hundreds of pieces of flaming wreckage smashed into the ground.

Catherine covered her head. She hadn't been in a warzone for thousands of years.

Hands grabbed her. Pulling her to her feet.

Drax and soldiers gathered around her. Bombs dropped around them.

Shattering the bodies of the soldiers.

Catherine rushed over to their corpses. Picking up their guns.

Catherine spun round.

Traitor baseline humans were storming towards them. Their superhumans masters had given them the foul task of getting the Artifact.

Something Catherine couldn't allow.

Catherine fired.

Heads exploded. Bodies shattered like glass. Catherine moved back to the Artifact.

It pulsed dark red.

Drax stood in front of her and Catherine spun around.

She had to get the Artifact moving. She needed a transport to get it to the cruiser.

Catherine placed her hands on the Artifact. She knew it wanted to react. It kept its promise.

Catherine started to move towards the bird-like shuttles that were landing around her.

Soldiers gathered around them to stop the enemy from destroying them.

Immense fireballs peppered around Catherine.

Flashes of immense heat almost burnt her skin.

Marines screamed around her. They were being slaughtered. She had to get the Artifact out.

Catherine saw Drax was walking quickly next to her.

The enemy was storming towards them. Chopping down loyalists like no tomorrow.

Catherine was running out of time.

A bomb smashed into the sand right in front of the Artifact.

Catherine was thrown backwards.

A massive explosion ripped across the battlefield.

Catherine looked up to see the cruiser was being hammered with enemy fire. Massive chunks of the ship were being smashed off it, ripped away like a child wanting to get to the present inside a gift.

Its engines destroyed.

Catherine screamed as the cruiser smashed into the sandy ground below. Exploding.

A shockwave started to rip towards her but the Artifact hummed and a solid wall of yellow, purple and pink sand formed in front of her and the other loyal forces.

The Artifact was protecting them.

A bullet ripped into Catherine's shoulder. She hissed.

Screams filled all around her as she heard the heads explode of her forces and she heard the searing of brains and the cooking of flesh filled her senses.

Then she saw the sight she had never ever wanted to see ever again.

Ten heavily armoured Angels of Death and Hope with crimson armour modelled on the armour of Knights from Old Earth stormed towards her.

Her traitorous children headed for the Artifact personally and as they stormed across the battlefield like the immortal gods that she created them as, Catherine's heart just sank.

She was frozen with utter fear as she watched her once proud creations snap the necks, shatter the heads and kill the loyalist forces that were basically no real threat to them so coldly.

They stormed towards her and the Artifact and even though they were wearing thick helmets, Catherine just knew they were surprised to see *her*.

Because the one thing she had never designed the Angels of Death and Hope with all their advance strength, power and resistance was for them to form parental attachments with her and the Emperor.

They normally served the Emperor unquestionably but she had never expected them to love, protect and treasure her like they did in those early ages.

The traitor superhumans stopped for the briefest of moments and just focused on her, then they simply waved at her and got back to their mission. Like all good soldiers were meant too.

Catherine was too shocked at the gesture to even will her body to do anything as the traitors attached a small teleportation unit to the Artifact.

The Artifact pulsed a final time in dark blue and it almost felt like a question of what should it do. Catherine was surprised that it was asking it more than anything else.

"Stay safe. Make sure I can find you. Because I will find you again," Catherine said.

The Artifact pulsed gently like that was exactly the loving answer that it wanted.

As the Artifact and the traitors teleported away, Catherine's blood ran cold and she had only just realised what a massive mistake this entire mission had truly been.

ANGELS OF MOTHER

CHAPTER 12

Even now Catherine had absolutely no idea if she was meant to be grateful or not that the superhuman traitors had decided to abandon the battle as soon as they had retrieved the Artifact. It was good in a way because it meant that reinforcements could attend to the wounded and thankfully Drax was alive but wounded.

But Catherine just wasn't sure how the hell she was meant to put a positive spin on such a failure of a mission.

Catherine stood perfectly straight in the bright sterile white medical bay of the blade-like warship she was in, and she just stared out of the massive floor-to-ceiling window. She couldn't tear her eyes away from the planet below with its constantly moving yellow, purple and pink sandy ground that seemed to have a life of its own.

Catherine knew that all of it was connected to the Artifact somehow, and as she heard the gentle breathing of Drax on the hovering metal slab behind her, Catherine was pleased that he was okay and alive and hopefully able to lead his military again soon. But

Catherine just had so many more questions than answers.

At least a few things were clear.

The Artifact was more powerful than anything she had seen for a long, long time. The superhuman traitors were obsessed with it and they had attacked an entire solar system just to get it, but the strangest thing was that in the far distance, across planets and hundreds of thousands of kilometres, Catherine could still see the bright flashes of cannon fire.

They were still here.

The traitors weren't leaving any time soon so neither was Catherine.

Catherine had come to this system searching for the Keystone and whatever else she had had the urge to find in the first place, she just couldn't leave without it. And the last thing she wanted was for the traitors to have such a devastating weapon in their hands.

Catherine turned around and saw Drax smiling at her and again probably dreaming about running his dirty fingers through her velvety blond hair, and whilst that would never happen. At least Catherine knew that she had friends here, injured friends but friends nonetheless.

So Catherine just smiled because if living for ninety thousand years had taught her anything, it was that patience was the ultimate weapon against the enemy.

Catherine could live forever and just wait for her traitorous creations to die, but there wasn't time for that. She needed to wait for her friends to heal themselves and get battle ready once more, and then and only then could she seek a way to get back her precious Artifact.

Because that was the truth of it. the Artifact was hers, and she wasn't going to let some dim-witted traitor or loyalist get their grubby little hands on it.

And that was a promise.

CHAPTER 13

The moons above shone like massive disco balls of pure sterile white light above the night-black sand of the planet, Doctor Catherine Taylor felt the icy coldness wrap around her like some kind of malicious blanket that pretended to protect her, but only actually wanted her dead.

Dead like the entire planet.

Catherine stood inside a little crater the size of most cities back on Old Earth with immense black slopes as steep as anything Catherine had ever seen before.

From what Catherine could see from where she stood to one side in the massive crater, there was something shining in the middle of the crater, she just hoped that was the Artifact she was seeking, but she couldn't bare the idea of exploring it just yet.

Just in case the enemy were watching her.

As much as she wanted to believe the cold, dead, ugly ground was just naturally black. That was far from the case, Catherine just knew that she was standing on the smashed-up remains of charred buildings, bodies and flora that once covered this luscious jungle world on the far edge of the Samuel System, one of the most remote systems in the Galactic South of the Great Human Empire. It was once so beautiful, stunning and just sheer perfection, but now it was only a mere husk of its former self.

Even the air smelt unnatural with almost suffocating hints of charred flesh, smouldering corpses and gunpowder filling the air like a veil designed to choke anyone who dared come to this planet of the traitors.

Yet Catherine wasn't scared of these superhumans.

Catherine hated the stupid plan that the commander in charge of the system's military, Commander Drax, had forced her to do in an effort to get back the delightful triangular Artifact that traitor superhumans had stolen from Catherine and the natives of the system.

Catherine was still so amazed, fearful and shocked that the superhuman Angels of Death and Hope that she had first created over 90,000 years ago had still turned traitor against the divine Emperor. Well that wasn't entirely fair to the three out of the nine legions of Angels that had stayed loyal to the Emperor.

It still broke Catherine's rather black heart, she had loved each and every one of her superhumans creations over the tens of thousands of years, and even though the Angel Project was basically self-running ever since, she still loved everyone who survived the process to become one of Catherine's Angels.

She had never told anyone, not even the glorious Emperor himself, about her feelings towards her creations and how guilty she felt about the traitors, and how badly she wished she could genetically engineer humans to never betray the Emperor.

But that was never ever going to be possible and Catherine just hated herself for it.

"Come in," Drax said over the communication network and through the earpiece in Catherine's left ear.

Catherine almost jumped at the sudden noise against the eerie silence of the planet.

"I'm here," Catherine said.

"Do you see the Artifact?" Drax asked.

Catherine slowly started walking across the massive crater towards the shining object in the middle of the crater. She was seriously glad that Drax was on the blade-like ship in high orbit with a full military detachment ready to go, if needed.

Catherine had laughed when Drax sounded like the military support wouldn't be needed, but if her traitorous children had invaded a system as unloved, forgettable and futile of the Samuel System then they were not going to part with the Artifact without an immense fight.

Even now as she went over to the shining object, Catherine was still puzzled to why Drax had only sent her in.

Her first idea had been because Drax wouldn't have minded her death but that was a lie, plain and simple, he liked her, and whilst Catherine didn't doubt that humans were messy and crazy and irrational creatures. She had absolutely no reason to suspect that Drax would actually want her death.

A few moments later Catherine got close enough to the shining object to thankfully confirm that the amazing twenty-metre-high, perfectly equilateral triangular object was the Artifact she was after.

The Artifact immediately pulsed with bright blue light like it was really glad to see an old friend again.

Catherine carefully went up to the Artifact and brushed her fingers carefully against the icy cold surface. Flashes of calming blue light danced over the Artifact's smooth surface, and Catherine was just glad it was okay, safe and alive.

But it was strange how the Artifact was perfectly intact without a single sign that the traitors had done anything to it. Catherine had seen the artifact retrievals before that her foul children had been involved in, and most artifacts were destroyed.

This one wasn't even dented during transport.

Catherine touched her earpiece. "Drax, I've found the object. Area is clear. Come down for extraction,"

The Artifact pulsed bright red.

"Aboard!" Catherine said out of reflex.

CHAPTER 14

Massive traitor superhumans teleported in around her. Their immense three-metre-tall frame dwarfing her.

Catherine knew that they were taller, stronger and deadlier than any human. It was exactly how she had created them but now she was surrounded by ten of them in a circle with their bright crimson armour styled on Knight Armour from Old Earth reflecting the sterile white light of the moons.

Fear gripped her.

These traitor superhumans could run twenty metres and kill her before she could ever think about screaming.

They could explode her head with their mass-explosive bullets from their guns the size of Catherine's head.

They could rip out her spine without her even able to contact Drax for help.

All these was exactly how she had designed her

Angels of Death and Hope so perfectly all those tens of thousands of years ago, and even though she didn't question herself, not even now with her death seemingly certain, she was starting to wonder if they would kill her quickly or slowly.

The tallest of the Traitor Superhumans who had a black stripe on his helmet marched over to Catherine. She strained her neck to look up at him through his bright red eye-slits on his helmet.

"Doctor," he said, his voice booming, slightly computerised but Catherine wasn't scared.

Most people might have collapsed in fear by now, but Catherine wasn't a normal human, as other people called her from time to time she was the Mother Of Angels.

"We are most grateful for your arrival. We were about to start testing the object without your guidance," the Leader said.

Catherine folded her arms. She had read report after report about her traitorous children and they were never this kind, they clearly needed something.

Catherine looked at the Artifact and again ran her fingers over its icy surface. The Artifact pulsed nervously.

"I'll protect you," Catherine said to the Artifact.

It didn't react, almost like it was questioning her ability to do it.

"We have the other artifact you know," the Leader said. "The ones the humans call the Keystone,"

Catherine absolutely failed to hide her surprise. The Keystone was a much smaller version of the Artifact, still triangular and made up from the same strange black metal, but she had purposefully left it on the system's capital world.

It was flat out impossible for the traitors to get it.

The Leader laughed. "You underestimate your children Doctor,"

Catherine's blood ran cold as she realised what he had said. They all knew they were her children, and she had never used the term *children* in front of anyone, occasionally the Emperor, but no one else. It was so strange to hear someone else call them, her children.

It was almost messed-up.

"You underestimate me Doctor," the Leader said. "You are aware of the Legions of your children that turned from your beloved Emperor?"

Catherine nodded and laughed. Of course she did, she was one of the brightest minds of the Great Human Empire, she constantly read, studied and learnt everything she could about the galaxy. So as soon as she had learnt about the traitors she had studied what Legions had turned traitor and which were loyal.

This particular Legion that these traitors belonged to with their crimson armour were possibly the worst of all the traitors. These belonged to the Lord of War's Legion, that had recently changed their name, to the Divine Children, Catherine hated the name almost as much as she hated the Lord Of War. Like all leaders of the Legions, Catherine had loved, protected and helped to train all 9 of them personally when the Angel Project first started.

And now that traitorous bastard child was leading the traitor forces against her beloved Emperor. A very costly mistake for them indeed.

"I know you're called the Divine Children," Catherine said. "But your legion is too well trained, clever and destructive to pull off a heist in secret against a Capital World, even if this system is so outdated in security,"

The Leader nodded and Catherine was sure if he took off his helmet he would have been smiling.

"Since when did the Raven Crow Legion join you?" Catherine asked.

Catherine had always had a soft spot for her superhuman spies that the Raven Crow Legion specialised in. In fact she absolutely loved each and every legion of the Angels for their unique talents and skills and abilities.

The Leader nodded slowly and waved his hand.

A moment later a small grey box teleported in and Catherine just knew that it was for her. So she slowly opened the warm metal box and she took out the smaller triangular Keystone.

As a scientist she had always wanted to put the two pieces together and see what would happen, and finally she would be able to.

Catherine held the Keystone in her hand and

looked at the Artifact. It didn't pulse at her, it didn't hesitate, it only felt like it was looking at Catherine in utter fear and undecidedness.

Catherine didn't even know if the Keystone and Artifact had ever been connected, or if the Artifact even knew what would happen.

The clicking of ten guns behind her made Catherine roll her eyes, the traitors wanted her to do this now.

Catherine slowly raised the Keystone up towards the middle of the Artifact's triangular centre where some of the metal seemingly magically melted away so she could place the Keystone inside.

Catherine wasn't sure she really wanted to do this but she was a scientist first and foremost, and her curiosity was definitely winning over her morality, like it always did.

She carefully placed the Keystone in the middle of the Artifact and nothing happened.

The Leader stood next to Catherine, and she was impressed her knees didn't fail her, she was basically standing next to a superhuman demigod.

The Artifact glowed blinding white.

Catherine shielded her eyes.

The entire planet banged, popped and vibrated.

An earthquake ripped through the planet.

Massive cracks appeared in the ground.

The Leader threw Catherine across the crater.

Then nothing.

CHAPTER 15

As Catherine jumped up she was surprised to see most of the ground around the Artifact had completely collapsed, and the Artifact was just floating there.

"Brilliant," the Leader said.

Catherine looked over to him too was standing a few metres from her, then she realised he was looking up and sadly the blade-like warship Drax was on was plumping towards the ground with thousands of escape pods launching, and every single flight-capable vehicle was zooming away too.

A few moments later Catherine heard the ear-splitting sound of the warship shattering, exploding and killing everyone silly enough to remain on board.

Catherine was alone now.

The Artifact glowed bright crimson and a small holographic control panel in a strange dead language appeared in front of Catherine.

She instantly knew what this was, the Artifact

was a weapon like no other, and it had chosen her to be its operator.

The clicking of ten superhuman guns sounded way too close for comfort and Catherine didn't dare look behind her.

Catherine swiped the control panel a few times and realised the Artifact had the power to strike at any planet in the entire Galaxy, and she saw on the very edges of the control panel, it was powerful enough to strike planets in other galaxies too, including Andromeda.

Catherine felt a cold superhuman hand on the back of her neck. A hand that could and would nicely snap it like The Leader wanted.

"The Lord of War will be most pleased. Now tell me Doctor how can I control it?" the Leader asked.

The Artifact pulsed violent red like that was the most insulting question it had ever heard, but that was the interesting thing. It clearly didn't want to serve the traitors, or maybe at all.

Catherine had encountered the Intelligence that existed inside the Keystone back on the Capital world, so maybe the Artifact was a kind of Super-Intelligence, artificial of course.

"I don't know," Catherine said.

The hand on the back of her neck tensed.

"I highly suggest you figure it out Doctor," the Leader said.

Catherine folded her arms and realised something she should have noticed earlier, why did the native humans insist on calling the smaller object a Keystone?

She had never ever asked Drax why they had called it that, she had always put it down to humans being silly, irrational or just plain stupid, but what if the native humans were telling the truth without truly knowing what they had discovered?

"Doctor," the Leader said, "do something?"

Catherine nodded and really focused on the holographic control panel in front of her, she had never seen the language before, she noticed a few features that allowed her to narrow it down to a type of language used by over twenty million different alien species over the past hundreds of millions of years.

Besides that she didn't know anything about the language. She was a geneticist not a linguist.

"Artifact," Catherine said, "are you definitely a weapon?"

The Artifact didn't respond.

Catherine felt the icy cold barrel of a superhuman gun pressed against the side of her head.

"Or are you a map?" Catherine asked.

The Artifact gingerly pulsed which Catherine took as a map, and she was starting to understand why the natives had called this a Keystone, or it was probably a corruption of a translation some historian had made when the Keystone was first discovered.

Catherine knew that this particular system of space had been home to an alien race known as the

Tau'Ra (Void Stones) before they were exterminated by another alien race about two thousand years before the very first humans evolved.

Catherine had studied the Tau'Ra language through the galactic south and their word *Kay'Ra*, didn't mean *Keystone*, it actually meant *Navigation Stone*, but so few knew that.

At least Catherine had finally worked out who had created the Keystone and the Artifact in the first place.

"The Tau'Ra made this," Catherine said. "And the Artifact is meant to lead us to something,"

The Leader pressed the gun barrel harder against her head. "Make it show us,"

The Artifact pulsed blood red light. Catherine had a feeling it didn't want to.

The Leader knocked Catherine aside. Whacking her to the ground.

The Leader grabbed the holographic control panel and started pressing buttons. It was clearly working for him.

"Targeting the entire system," the Leader said.

"Stop!" Catherine shouted.

The Artifact hummed louder and louder.

"You'll destroy everything. Billions will die," Catherine said.

The superhumans laughed. The other superhumans trained their guns on Catherine.

"Targeted!" the Leader shouted.

The Artifact caused another earthquake. Massive

chunks of ground shattered. Splitting the planet.

Bullets screamed through the air.

Denting superhuman armour.

Humans roared towards Catherine. She spun around.

Black armoured marines stormed towards her. Loyalist forces were alive.

Blade-like fighters zoomed overhead. Bird-like shuttles roared into the crater. Troopers charged out of them.

The superhumans fired. Their bullets ripping chunks of flesh out from the marines.

Catherine flew at the Leader.

Catching him off guard. Tackling him to the ground.

He slapped her. Punched her in the stomach.

Then he stopped. His hands shook. Maybe out of fear. Maybe out of guilt. Maybe out of utter sadness at striking his mother.

A missile struck the Leader. Sending him flying.

Catherine didn't have time to react. She raced over to the control panel. She had to stop the Artifact.

It stopped working to her touch. It wasn't listening to her. The Artifact didn't love her anymore.

It had found a new Master.

The Artifact buzzed. The air crackled with electrical energy.

The Artifact flew at Catherine.

She jumped to one side. The Artifact almost

killed her.

Catherine saw dead marines at her feet. She picked up their weapons.

Firing at the Artifact. It charged at her. Catherine rolled to one side.

Catherine fired more at the Artifact.

It didn't even dent it.

The Artifact glowed dark crimson. It was about to fire.

Catherine charged at it.

She jumped into the air.

Thrusting out her fist.

Her fist slamming into the Keystone in the middle of the Artifact.

The Keystone smashed out of the Artifact and the Artifact shattered.

Catherine just watched in utter wonder as the strange black metal the Artifact was made out of turned to fine black dust, then it rose up revealing a set of coordinates, and an image of a massive straight circle in space.

Catherine didn't know what the image was trying to show her but it was clearly a disc of some kind, and she just knew that it was a weapon of some kind.

Then the black dust that made up the image simply disappeared and as Catherine heard her traitorous children teleport away, she was just left there wondering a simple question.

Who was going to make it to the disc first? Her or her foul children?

CHAPTER 16

About two hours later Catherine stood in a very bright white oval chamber with smooth sterile walls and a massive holographic table in the middle, showing her the exact coordinate that the Artifact had revealed to her.

The entire chamber smelt of harsh lemon, lime and grapefruit from harsh cleaning chemicals from the blade-like destroyer spaceship's automatic cleaning sensors, that left the wonderful taste of key lime pie on her tongue. The very best of pies.

Catherine just stood there in complete silence as she watched the massive bright blue disc that was the same size as some moons just sit there in space like it was nothing.

Commander Drax had already gathered a fleet now that the traitors had abandoned the Samuel System and were making all due haste towards the coordinates. Catherine just wanted to beat them there but she knew that was an impossibility now.

Catherine had never seen anything like the disc before because it looked so strange. It literally was just a disc, it didn't show any weapons, signs of life or anything else to suggest it was capable of being important.

But no alien race, especially the Tau'Ra, would have gone to lengths this great to hide the disc, if it wasn't dangerous or important.

As Catherine just stood there allowing her eyes to solely focus on the hologram and actually know what bright light was once more after being on that planet's dark surface for so long, she just couldn't believe what her children had become.

The traitors were still monsters that burned entire worlds, killed every living thing that moved and wanted to kill billions of innocent humans for no reason, but they had showed emotion at hurting her.

That might become the most important finding of her entire trip to the Samuel System, but with the prize for everyone in sight, Catherine just knew that her foul children wouldn't hesitate to kill her if it meant getting the disc for the Lord of War, their leader, and his apocalyptic plans for enslaving humanity.

CHAPTER 17

Catherine Taylor stood patiently on a very hard metal surface at the very edge of a massive metallic blue disc that seemed to stretch on endlessly. She didn't like how the immense disc seemed perfectly flat despite it looking like it had metal mountain ranges, lakes and other natural features from orbit.

Catherine wasn't even sure what the disc actually was, all she knew that was through the harsh oxygen-recycler firmly attached to her face, was that the air stunk of iron, copper and left a foul taste of blood on her tongue.

The bright moons, stars and nearby planets seem to sparkle like stunning jewels against the dark blackness of space as Catherine studied how the light affected the disc. Most of the time the light was simply absorbed, not reflected by the strange blue metal of the disc. That was flat out weird in itself but it didn't happen.

The longer Catherine stood there studying and

making sure to take in as much as the disc as possible, the icier her skin got, despite her wearing an envirosuit that was humming louder in some vain effort to warm up her body.

After weeks of chasing down artifacts, hunting down clues to the mystery of the Keystone and more, Catherine was so glad to finally be standing where everything had led her to.

But she was equally confused at what this disc actually was. Was it a weapon? A city? A graveyard?

Catherine had no idea but she seriously looked forward to finding out, especially since she was one of the few minds in the Great Human Empire that possibly could solve the mystery, considering she had been alive for over 90,000 years. Thanks to her mastery of genetics, advanced medical and rejuvenation treatments.

The only comfort Catherine found in the entire situation was the little fact that the traitor superhuman Angels of Death and Hope hadn't made it to the disc before she had.

Catherine was more than glad about that, she might have created the Angels for the Emperor as superhuman soldiers 90,000 years ago, but she hated herself for creating them with the possibility of treachery.

Catherine just hoped they never turned up.

The sound of distant banging made Catherine roll her eyes as she slightly turned to see Commander Drax, the person in charge of the unloved and very forgettable Samuel System's military, and five heavily armed Empire Army soldiers walk towards her as they departed their blade-like shuttle.

With their goal so close, Catherine was actually starting to appreciate Drax a little more with his mind, attention to detail and he still clearly liked her. Catherine couldn't blame him, it seemed that tons of men loved her short blond hair that looked so lifeful and seductive, but Catherine was going to make sure nothing ever happened between her and Drax.

"What is this place?" Drax asked.

Catherine carefully took out a small handheld scanning device out of a backpack she was carrying, and she started to scan the surface and the air and whatever else the scanner picked up.

The results were beyond strange to say the least.

"Air is a combination of nitrogen and hydrogen. Basically no oxygen," Catherine said.

Now she was even more glad she was wearing the enviro-suit but if it ripped even by a millimetre then she would be dead. She had to be careful.

"Air also shows high concentrations of Nanobots, flesh eating capabilities, probably some kind of defence mechanism," Catherine said.

Catherine just smiled as she saw some of the Empire Army troopers hesitate and move uncomfortably. Catherine had absolutely no doubt that there was something grand hidden here, but if those Nanobots activated then she just had a feeling that they could rip through the Enviro-suits in seconds.

That wasn't good.

"What was this place meant to be protecting?" Drax asked.

Catherine didn't care for the question so she simply started walking forward. If there was anything to find on the strange disc then it was most likely to be at the centre.

But something was seriously bothering her. In her 90,000 years Catherine had studied tons of alien cultures and races, but very few of them had had the technology to create flesh-eating Nanobots, so who created the disc?

In finding the location of the disc, Catherine had run across the now-extinct alien race known as the Tau'Ra, who had seemingly built the artifacts that led her to this disc. But she had never seen anything suggesting they had Nanobots of all things.

Sure the Tau'Ra were able to create spaceships, warships and amazing weapons that had allowed them to forge a small empire for themselves in far, far galactic south, but nanobots seemed a stretch for them.

What if humans made them?

Catherine stopped dead in her tracks. What if the traitor superhumans, her foul traitorous children, had actually gotten here first?

Screams ripped through the air.

Catherine spun around.

Catherine just watched in utter horror as the

nanobots activated and ripped into the soft juicy flesh of the five heavily armed soldiers with her and Drax. Their enviro-suits became shreds, their blood became a thick mist that thirsty nanobots drank up as quick as they could, and then they stunk their nano-teeth into the delicious human flesh.

Catherine just looked at Drax as ten superhumans teleported in around them wearing night-black armour based on the Knights from Old Earth.

"Doctor!" the Leader shouted.

CHAPTER 18

Catherine just rolled her eyes, this wasn't good, especially as when the Leader had hurt her before he was clearly shaken by it, but she just knew that feeling was gone now.

Given the chance he would kill her.

The other nine superhumans fixed their superhuman guns, capable of explosively ripping her body to atoms with a single bullet, on Catherine and Drax.

Catherine just needed to buy herself some time to figure out a great idea to get away. She just hoped beyond hope that this Disc was similar to the artifacts that led her here, because those Artifacts seemed alive and wanted to protect her.

She just hoped this disc was capable of similar intelligence.

"I presume you want me to show you how this disc works?" Catherine asked.

The Leader went over to Catherine and gestured

her to walk with him.

Catherine did as he wished, it was best just to keep him happy at this point, and she continued walking over the endless blue metal surface of the disc. Still not seeing any of the mountain ranges, lakes and other natural features she had seen from orbit.

"What happened to the natural features Doctor?" the Leader asked.

Catherine subtly checked if Drax was still behind her and he thankfully was, along with the nine other traitor superhumans, in a perfect straight line, making sure Drax didn't try anything.

"I don't know but what capabilities has your ships got? Science labs? Scanners? Atmospheric detectors?" Catherine asked.

She probably made up the last one but she didn't care at this point.

The Leader huffed as he seemed to step over something that Catherine couldn't see.

"What area of the light spectrum are you operating at?" Catherine asked.

She had always designed her beloved superhuman Angels to be stronger, tougher and deadlier than any baseline humans, but she had almost forgotten about her children's ability to see outside the normal light spectrum.

"Outside your range," the Leader said.

Catherine stopped.

Catherine gestured if it was okay for her to get something out of her backpack, the Leader nodded, and Catherine quickly tested the gravitational pull of the disc with a small blade-like scanner.

It was so strange that the superhuman seemed able to see things that Catherine couldn't, but what was even stranger was she didn't have to step over things, but the Leader seemingly had to.

"What did you step over earlier?" Catherine asked.

"A small stream, you walked in," the Leader said.

Catherine turned to see Drax and even now the nine superhumans weren't in a perfectly straight line like they were earlier. It was almost like they were trying to avoid standing in something.

"You're avoiding a hole in the disc that... your commander is standing in," the Leader said.

Catherine smiled. This was amazing, clearly there was light reflecting somewhere on the light spectrum and telling the superhumans that there was something there, but in reality there wasn't. Not that she could see it anyway.

The little blade-like scanner beeped and Catherine was surprised to see that she was standing between two gravitational fields. It was so slight which was why Catherine didn't feel anything, but it was starting to make sense.

"I think there's more than one gravitational force acting on the disc. Clearly artificial in nature," Catherine said. "But I believe there is enough of a gravitational difference that it pulls the light waves apart, making it difficult to see what's really going on,"

Even though the superhumans were wearing helmets, Catherine just knew they weren't buying it.

"I designed you all so you could see what other humans couldn't," Catherine said. "I hardwired your brains to reconnect light waves in case there was ever a battlefield like this,"

The Leader slowly nodded.

Catherine clicked her fingers. "We're on a hologram. That's why Drax isn't falling through the hole in the ground and why I'm not tripping over the stream or anything. It's because they aren't real and most importantly they're holograms and then the light showing them is being ripped apart,"

The Leader folded his arms and gestured they keep walking.

Catherine nodded.

"Then why can we see things from Orbit?" the Leader asked.

"Because it must be perspective related. It's advance things, but clearly the gravitational force of the disc has realigned the light waves at some point,"

Someone screamed.

More people screamed.

Four of the superhumans fell into the disc.

The Leader grabbed Catherine. She heard her suit tensing. It was so close to ripping.

Catherine was going to die.

"What was that?"

The Leader froze. The other superhumans froze.

Catherine felt her enviro-suit tense and she couldn't move anymore. Drax was probably the same.

CHAPTER 19

The entire landscape shifted, twirled and swirled as Catherine found herself in a brand-new environment, it took her eyes a few moments to adjust to the awful light but she was in some kind of jet-black cave made from black metal.

The only light in the entire cave seemed to be coming from a roaring, crackling and talking fire in the dead centre of it, just a few metres from her.

Catherine felt no warmth from the fire and her enviro-suit shut up and a gentle wind ripped it off her, but it didn't hurt in the slightest.

Catherine did have to walk about a metre though to pick up her backpack and she carefully placed it back on her back. There was no way she wasn't having that equipment close to her.

And for some reason, Catherine could breathe perfectly fine. The air smelt fresh with hints of jasmine, clove and pine that seemed so unnatural for the harshness of the cave.

The fire crackled intensely before a very tall being rose out of the fire and simply stood there.

Catherine had never seen anything like it in her entire long life, the being had eight long scaly legs with scales made up of what looked like black metal with small amounts of bright fiery blood (or something similar) running through it. Its head was like a beetle's and its body was so short and fat, Catherine couldn't see if it was a simple chest or if it was made up of other sections like a spider's.

But she recognised the rough body shape from strange drawings that scientists had discovered in caves over the centuries.

She was looking at a very much alive Tau'Ra.

"You aren't a very rich Tau'Ra," Catherine said. "Tau'Ra were meant to be the most beautiful creatures in the galaxy at one point, they were not meant to be foul abominations,"

Catherine didn't know why she was being so insulting but she was more concerned about Drax's safety than herself. She couldn't see Drax.

"Doctor," someone said through the darkness.

It took a few moments to realise it was the Leader's voice, it was in pain and clearly all the other superhumans and hopefully Drax was down here too.

"You are a geneticist?" the Leader asked.

Catherine quickly realised that the Tau'Ra was having to use the Leader to talk to her, understandable considering it would never have the voice-box required to create the sounds and pitches needed for the human tongue.

"I am," Catherine said.

"Doctor? I need you to help me,"

Catherine shook her head and went over to the Tau'Ra creature. The closer she got the more she realised that there was nothing natural about this creature.

On each of its joints there was a massive defect with the muscles that moved the leg seemingly coming harder and more like stone, on its bright red eyes they seemed to be burnt and damaged, and even its body or chest seemed to be afflicted with some kind of decay.

No wonder it needed the constant heat and purifying nature of the fire.

Catherine bit her lip as she had seen this all before, all 90,000 years ago when her first Angels had gone so wrong, and their genetics were as faulty as anything she had ever seen. She had created monsters back then.

And someone had clearly created a monster now.

Then Catherine realised the true purpose of the disc. It wasn't a weapon, a city or anything like the artifacts had remotely suggested. Sure the artifacts might have had the capability to steal the power of entire worlds, but it was now clear that those capabilities were meant to kill off people that were searching for the disc.

The disc was actually a prison of sorts, a storage area for the foul creations of the Tau'Ra or something or maybe the other Tau'Ra were meant to be creating a cure before their extinction stopped their critical work.

Catherine explained her theory to the creature and it nodded slowly.

As much as Catherine wanted to help and actually felt sorry for the creature, she couldn't help it. It might have been a stunning research opportunity but she had studied Tau'Ra genetics thousands of years ago after a historian friend gifted her a DNA sample for her birthday (much to the utter fury of the infamous Plutonian geneticists), and Tau'Ra DNA was impossible to work with.

The DNA was so unstable, difficult to separate and it was just so difficult to manipulate that it wasn't actually worth the effort to do so.

Catherine was about to tell the creature that when it dawned on her that if she said that, the Creature would probably kill her.

And as much as she hated the very concept of her traitorous children being able to help her, she just knew that them and Drax were her only hope. She was a scientist, not a fighter.

She just hoped that the traitors would help her and not kill her.

A choice she seriously didn't want to bet her life on.

CHAPTER 20

"I will help you if you free my friends," Catherine said.

The last word burnt Catherine's tongue like acid, she hated herself for even considering her traitorous children friends, but she was running out of time.

The creature seemed to stretch its neck in confusion. It didn't want to but it was weighing up its opportunities.

Catherine subtly felt around in her little backpack, in case she felt a weapon, she sometimes packed one but she had rarely felt the need for it before.

"No doctor," the Leader said. "I will not release them,"

Catherine rolled her eyes, now she was well and truly on her own.

Catherine found a small knife she always carried in case she needed to slice a sample of mummified flesh, but this time she only needed to kill a creature in fire.

"Kill her," the Leader said.

Catherine heard the superhumans move towards her. Drax was coming too. They were going to kill her.

Catherine charged forward. Rushing towards the Tau'Ra.

It looked confused.

Catherine jumped into the air.

Drax tackled her to the ground. He punched her in the head.

Catherine whacked him round the face. Drax fell off. Catherine jumped up.

She raced to the Tau'Ra creature.

The Leader tackled her. His superhuman strength choked her.

Catherine stared through his helmet. She willed him to remember she was his mother.

His superhuman hands tightened round her throat.

Drax tackled the Leader to the ground. He had recovered.

The Leader seemed to recover. His hands shook in horror about attacking Catherine.

It only took an injury for the captured superhumans to recover.

Catherine charged at the Tau'Ra. It screamed.

Catherine leapt into the air.

Thrusting her knife into the Tau'Ra eye.

Its head imploded, Drax grabbed Catherine away

from the fire as she landed and the Tau'Ra screamed as the flames engulfed it.

The entire disc roared, popped and banged.

"The Disc is moving," the Leader said.

Catherine just looked at Drax. They were trapped. The traitors could teleport away, they couldn't.

The superhumans grabbed her and Drax and teleported away.

ANGELS OF MOTHER

CHAPTER 21

Catherine flat out couldn't believe it as the traitors rematerialised in the oval bridge with rows upon rows of holographic computers lining the bridge of Drax's warships, they threw down Catherine and Drax and teleported off again.

"Traitor warships haloing," a tall Captain in black uniform said.

"Put them through," Catherine ordered.

The Captain did what was said as Drax slowly stood up.

"Doctor," the Leader said. "We must fire on the Disc together,"

Catherine completely agreed. If there were other Tau'Ra on the disc then they had to be destroyed.

"Fire!" Catherine shouted.

The entire warship screamed to life as it fired every single missile, gun and cannon at the disc.

Within moments it shattered into billions of tiny fragments and massive bodies of Tau'Ra abominations looked like they were screaming in silent terror as the coldness of space froze them, and the moment they smashed into a group of tiny fragments of the disc.

Their bodies shattered.

"Traitor fleet is escaping," the Captain said. "Orders?"

Catherine simply looked at Drax. She wasn't going to order the warship to attack the traitors that had saved her life, no matter what the cost was further down the line.

"Leave them," Drax said firmly. "Return to the Samuel system at all due haste,"

***

An hour later, Catherine sat at a very large bright grey desk that hovered perfectly above the ground in a sterile white rectangular room that Drax had given her as a little office whilst they were travelling to and from the Samuel System in search of the disc. Catherine had kept it relatively impersonal and kept it rather minimal with no the other furniture but that was exactly how she liked things.

Catherine had only allowed two small armchairs that faced her across the desk, a slate coffee table and a small red sofa on the far end of the office for the sake of comfort when she really, really needed it.

At least the enviro-systems on the ship were working better than the ones she had smelt before on ships from the Samuel System, with its delightful hints of rosemary, thyme and freshly-made lemonade.

It was a rather wonderful sensation after the weirdest of the disc and the Tau'Ra.

Thankfully, it hadn't taken too long for Catherine to write up her report to send to Earth so the other military and scientists could at least acknowledge her findings, and what else had happened.

She was seriously hoping the military and other leaders in the Empire would overlook her letting the traitors help her and the fact that Drax had allowed the traitor fleet to escape.

Sure she wouldn't sleep easy tonight because she would be constantly concerned about how many worlds those particular traitors would burn, people they would kill and whatever other dark plots they would be able to take part in because they were alive, and not dead.

But Catherine stood by her decision, the traitors had helped them escape with their lives, and they hadn't fired on Catherine's warship, so chances are they would be executed when they returned to their leader the Lord of War anyway.

So the traitors would die regardless.

The metal office door slid open and Drax walked in, wearing a rather tasteless dark uniform that Catherine supposed was his version of casual "evening" wear and he walked towards her holding a tray. Judging by the smell, and it was only confirmed when he placed the tray on her desk along with a coffee pot and two mugs, he was bringing them both some richly sweetly spiced coffee that the Samuel

System was definitely not famous for.

"Thank you," Catherine said as Drax poured her a mug.

It smelt amazing.

"Here's to our mission and our time together," Drax said as they cheered their mugs together.

Catherine just nodded and this really was the end of their time together. Catherine had only been in the Samuel System for a few months, searching and hunting and studying down links between the artifacts and the massive disc they had eventually led her to.

Catherine had come here because she had felt the urge that something important was here, almost like a mystery that she needed to solve desperately.

And now she had actually done it, Catherine felt so relieved, wonderful and much lighter than she had been when she first came here.

"Thank you, truly," Catherine said, "for all your help. I will make sure Empire High Command hears of your bravery, actions and dedication to Him On Earth,"

Drax smiled like a schoolboy at the idea of the Emperor himself being told about him.

"What will you do now?" Drax asked.

Catherine just only smiled like a schoolgirl herself. There was so many amazing research opportunities, ancient and future cultures to study and so many different ways to help the war effort against the alien, traitors and mutants that she had no idea what to do next.

But one first was certain.

No matter what happened next in Catherine's long life, she was always going to serve her glorious divine Emperor in some effort to save, protect and love humanity from all the threats it faced in an uncaring galaxy.

"Doc?" Drax asked.

Catherine just smiled. "I'll travel north once more. I'll travel back to the core of the Milky Way and set off from there once more. My life is about serving the glorious Emperor so my research projects find me. I may have to search a while but I will find another project soon enough and I cannot wait to see where that will take me,"

Drax gave her a weak smile, and now Catherine was starting to realise that he did actually care about her a lot. Not just from a romantic viewpoint, but as a person too.

Drax had never been born or from or cared about the Samuel System above his service to Emperor, so being military commander of a forgotten solar system was behind him. Drax deserved so much more than Catherine had ever given him credit for.

Catherine just rolled her eyes. "I will talk with Empire High Command and get you transferred out of here if you want. I have that sort of influence and we need more men like you on the frontline,"

Drax smiled and Catherine wondered if his face was about to break it was so large.

"Thank you," Drax shouted.

Drax started to get up and he was probably going to celebrate the news, because she really did have that sort of influence after gifting the Empire with the Angels of Death and Hope.

"Commander," Catherine said, "I will warn you though, there will be a reckoning for our actions today. There are many that will not see too kindly to us allowing traitor superhumans to get away,"

Drax simply nodded and left.

As Catherine just sat at her desk taking a sensational lightly spiced mouthful of the amazing coffee, she really couldn't stop thinking about the reckoning that was bound to happen at some point.

She could be arrested, trialled or killed for her so-called treason against the Emperor, but she doubted He would ever allow that.

But it was still a possibility.

No one mattered in the bitter end, Catherine still had time and she was going to make damn well sure she used every single second of it preciously.

Catherine was going to help humanity win the war, protect themselves and hopefully ensure their extinction was an impossibility.

And that search and quest for knowledge made her happier than any sane woman had the right to feel, because she simply absolutely loved her job, Empire and most importantly her divine Emperor.

GET YOUR FREE SHORT STORY NOW!
And get signed up to Connor Whiteley's newsletter to hear about new gripping books, offers and exciting projects. (You'll never be sent spam)
https://www.subscribepage.com/garrosignup

About the author:

Connor Whiteley is the author of over 60 books in the sci-fi fantasy, nonfiction psychology and books for writer's genre and he is a Human Branding Speaker and Consultant.

He is a passionate warhammer 40,000 reader, psychology student and author.

Who narrates his own audiobooks and he hosts The Psychology World Podcast.

All whilst studying Psychology at the University of Kent, England.

Also, he was a former Explorer Scout where he gave a speech to the Maltese President in August 2018 and he attended Prince Charles' 70th Birthday Party at Buckingham Palace in May 2018.

Plus, he is a self-confessed coffee lover!

Other books by Connor Whiteley:

Bettie English Private Eye Series
A Very Private Woman
The Russian Case
A Very Urgent Matter
A Case Most Personal
Trains, Scots and Private Eyes
The Federation Protects
Cops, Robbers and Private Eyes
Just Ask Bettie English
An Inheritance To Die For
The Death of Graham Adams
Bearing Witness
The Twelve
The Wrong Body
The Assassination Of Bettie English
Wining And Dying
Eight Hours
Uniformed Cabal
A Case Most Christmas

Gay Romance Novellas
Breaking, Nursing, Repairing A Broken Heart
Jacob And Daniel
Fallen For A Lie
Spying And Weddings
Clean Break

Awakening Love
Meeting A Country Man
Loving Prime Minister
Snowed In Love
Never Been Kissed
Love Betrays You

Lord of War Origin Trilogy:
Not Scared Of The Dark
Madness
Burn Them All

The Fireheart Fantasy Series
Heart of Fire
Heart of Lies
Heart of Prophecy
Heart of Bones
Heart of Fate

City of Assassins (Urban Fantasy)
City of Death
City of Martyrs
City of Pleasure
City of Power

Agents of The Emperor
Return of The Ancient Ones
Vigilance
Angels of Fire
Kingmaker
The Eight
The Lost Generation
Hunt
Emperor's Council
Speaker of Treachery
Birth Of The Empire
Terraforma
Spaceguard

The Rising Augusta Fantasy Adventure Series
Rise To Power
Rising Walls
Rising Force
Rising Realm

Lord Of War Trilogy (Agents of The Emperor)
Not Scared Of The Dark
Madness
Burn It All Down

Miscellaneous:
RETURN
FREEDOM
SALVATION
Reflection of Mount Flame
The Masked One
The Great Deer
English Independence

OTHER SHORT STORIES BY CONNOR WHITELEY

Mystery Short Story Collections
Criminally Good Stories Volume 1: 20 Detective Mystery Short Stories
Criminally Good Stories Volume 2: 20 Private Investigator Short Stories
Criminally Good Stories Volume 3: 20 Crime Fiction Short Stories
Criminally Good Stories Volume 4: 20 Science Fiction and Fantasy Mystery Short Stories
Criminally Good Stories Volume 5: 20 Romantic Suspense Short Stories

Mystery Short Stories:
Protecting The Woman She Hated
Finding A Royal Friend
Our Woman In Paris
Corrupt Driving
A Prime Assassination
Jubilee Thief
Jubilee, Terror, Celebrations
Negative Jubilation
Ghostly Jubilation
Killing For Womenkind
A Snowy Death
Miracle Of Death
A Spy In Rome
The 12:30 To St Pancreas
A Country In Trouble
A Smokey Way To Go
A Spicy Way To GO
A Marketing Way To Go
A Missing Way To Go
A Showering Way To Go
Poison In The Candy Cane
Kendra Detective Mystery Collection Volume 1
Kendra Detective Mystery Collection Volume 2
Mystery Short Story Collection Volume 1

ANGELS OF MOTHER

Mystery Short Story Collection Volume 2
Criminal Performance
Candy Detectives
Key To Birth In The Past

<u>Science Fiction Short Stories:</u>
Their Brave New World
Gummy Bear Detective
The Candy Detective
What Candies Fear
The Blurred Image
Shattered Legions
The First Rememberer
Life of A Rememberer
System of Wonder
Lifesaver
Remarkable Way She Died
The Interrogation of Annabella Stormic
Blade of The Emperor
Arbiter's Truth
Computation of Battle
Old One's Wrath
Puppets and Masters
Ship of Plague
Interrogation
Edge of Failure

Fantasy Short Stories:
City of Snow
City of Light
City of Vengeance
Dragons, Goats and Kingdom
Smog The Pathetic Dragon
Don't Go In The Shed
The Tomato Saver
The Remarkable Way She Died
Dragon Coins
Dragon Tea
Dragon Rider

All books in 'An Introductory Series':
Careers In Psychology
Psychology of Suicide
Dementia Psychology
Clinical Psychology Reflections Volume 4
Forensic Psychology of Terrorism And Hostage-Taking
Forensic Psychology of False Allegations
Year In Psychology
CBT For Anxiety
CBT For Depression
Applied Psychology
BIOLOGICAL PSYCHOLOGY 3RD EDITION

COGNITIVE PSYCHOLOGY THIRD EDITION
SOCIAL PSYCHOLOGY- 3RD EDITION
ABNORMAL PSYCHOLOGY 3RD EDITION
PSYCHOLOGY OF RELATIONSHIPS- 3RD EDITION
DEVELOPMENTAL PSYCHOLOGY 3RD EDITION
HEALTH PSYCHOLOGY
RESEARCH IN PSYCHOLOGY
A GUIDE TO MENTAL HEALTH AND TREATMENT AROUND THE WORLD- A GLOBAL LOOK AT DEPRESSION
FORENSIC PSYCHOLOGY
THE FORENSIC PSYCHOLOGY OF THEFT, BURGLARY AND OTHER CRIMES AGAINST PROPERTY
CRIMINAL PROFILING: A FORENSIC PSYCHOLOGY GUIDE TO FBI PROFILING AND GEOGRAPHICAL AND STATISTICAL PROFILING.
CLINICAL PSYCHOLOGY
FORMULATION IN PSYCHOTHERAPY
PERSONALITY PSYCHOLOGY AND INDIVIDUAL DIFFERENCES
CLINICAL PSYCHOLOGY

REFLECTIONS VOLUME 1
CLINICAL PSYCHOLOGY
REFLECTIONS VOLUME 2
Clinical Psychology Reflections Volume 3
CULT PSYCHOLOGY
Police Psychology

A Psychology Student's Guide To University
How Does University Work?
A Student's Guide To University And Learning
University Mental Health and Mindset

www.ingramcontent.com/pod-product-compliance
Lightning Source LLC
LaVergne TN
LVHW012120070526
838202LV00056B/5800